Secrets of the Sequoias

Adventures with the Parkers

by Mike Graf

illustrations by
Joyce Mihran Turley

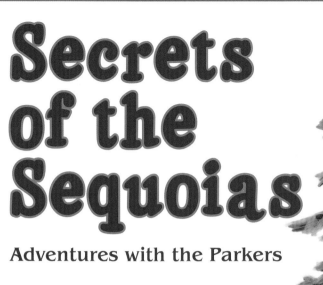

FARCOUNTRY
PRESS

PHOTO CREDITS:

ISBN: 978-1-56037-656-9

© 2016 by Farcountry Press
Text © 2016 by Mike Graf
Illustrations © Joyce Mihran Turley

For more information about our books, write Farcountry Press, P.O. Box 5630, Helena, MT 59604; call (800) 821-3874; or visit www.farcountrypress.com.

 Produced and printed in the United States of America.

20 19 18 17 16   1 2 3 4 5

1

"The secret of the sequoia," the Grant Grove Ranger explained, "is for seeds to sprout in the right location. And the biggest trees like the General Grant did all the right things. They sprouted in the best combination of sunlight, moisture, and nutrients."

And with that the ranger said, "C'mon, let's go see the second largest tree in the world."

The Parker family, along with a large group of people, were on the Grant Grove guided walk in Kings Canyon National Park. They followed the ranger to the General Grant Tree. As the group approached the immense, towering sequoia, one older man looked at the giant trees all around and said, "I'm just over-come with emotion. These trees have been here for so long and they're so large. Our lives seem incredibly small by comparison."

Another person added, "I can totally sense the need that people

The Top Ten Largest Trees in the World by Volume

Sequoias are the largest trees in the world. California coastal redwoods grow taller, but in sheer volume, the sequoia tops them all. Other large trees worldwide include: cypress, kauri, Sitka spruce, Douglas-fir, and red cedar.

The ten largest sequoia trees are all in California, the only place where sequoias grow naturally. Here they are, with their trunk volume measured in cubic feet:

1) General Sherman: 52,508
2) General Grant: 46,608
3) President: 45,148
4) Lincoln: 44,471
5) Stagg: 42,557
6) Boole: 42,272
7) Genesis: 41,897
8) Franklin: 41,280
9) King Arthur: 40,656
10) Monroe: 40,104

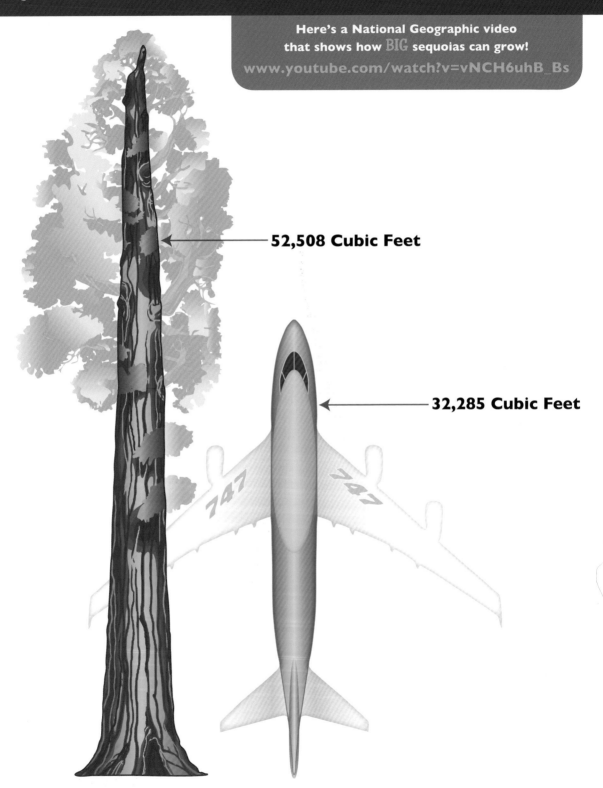

Here's a National Geographic video that shows how BIG sequoias can grow!
www.youtube.com/watch?v=vNCH6uhB_Bs

52,508 Cubic Feet

32,285 Cubic Feet

before us must have felt to preserve and protect them."

Soon the ranger stopped the group in front of the General Grant. He looked up at the massive sequoia and then toward the gathered visitors. "Pretty amazing, isn't it? Almost hard to believe. In fact, early visitors had a hard time convincing people in other parts of the country and the world that these trees were real."

"But they are very real. Three of the first four national parks in the world were preserved in part because of giant sequoias. First there was Yellowstone, established on March 1, 1872. But there are no sequoias in Yellowstone. The second national park was Sequoia National Park, set aside on September 25, 1890. A week later, congress also preserved Yosemite which has three sequoia groves, and Kings Canyon, where we are standing, as new national parks on October 1, 1890. This park was first named after our massive tree here and called General Grant National Park. Later the boundaries were increased and the whole area became Kings Canyon National Park on March 4, 1940."

The ranger paused for a moment and gazed up again at the massive sequoia, obviously awestruck by its immensity even though he had seen it many times. "The Grant Tree is the second largest tree in the world based on the volume of its trunk. But a few years ago, scientists carefully measured not just the

trunk but the branches too. They found that if branches are included in volume, then the President's Tree in Sequoia National Park is actually larger. So the Grant Tree here is either the second or third largest tree, depending on how you measure it." Then the ranger took off his hat and said, "Let me show you something. All national park rangers wear hats that have sequoia cones on their leather hat bands." Pointing to his belt, he added, "They are also stamped on our belts. The sequoia is a symbol of our national parks. It is a big deal!"

The people in the group looked from the ranger, then back to the General Grant. "By the way," the ranger continued, "this is also the 'Nation's Christmas Tree.' People come out here every year in December to celebrate the holidays with the General Grant."

The ranger offered more insights about the tree standing before them. "A sequoia grows upward for about the first 600 years of its life until it reaches its full height. After that, it doesn't grow any taller but continues to grow larger in diameter the rest of its life."

Dad grabbed the small bulge that had gradually appeared in recent years around his waist. "I sure know what that's like."

GENERAL GRANT
THE NATION'S CHRISTMAS TREE

In 1924, R. J. Senior of Sanger, California, was visiting General Grant National Park and the General Grant Tree. A little girl was standing by while they were both admiring the Grant Tree. The girl exclaimed, "What a wonderful Christmas tree it would be." The idea stayed with Mr. Senior, and by the very next year a Christmas program was held right at the General Grant Tree on Christmas Day. The General Grant Tree was officially designated the "Nation's Christmas Tree" on April 28th, 1926. The label and an annual holiday trek to the tree continues today.

2

The next day, the Parkers—twins Morgan and James and their parents Kristen and Robert—drove to the Redwood Canyon trailhead and started hiking on the Sugar Bowl Trail. They left a forested area scattered with many mature sequoias and hiked onto a ridge with an open view of Redwood Canyon below. Morgan was the first to point out the clumps of giant trees near the bottom of the canyon. "There are sequoias down there!" she exclaimed. "A whole bunch of them."

Dad responded. "They sure have that rounded, broccoli-shaped top."

The family continued hiking down several switchbacks. They moved slowly on the rocky terrain, their backpacks riding heavily on their hips and shoulders. Soon they were back in the shade of the deep forest. And after

that, the giant trees were everywhere along the trail.

Mom spoke with awe. "Of all our journeys, this one is certainly special! Now we get to camp overnight in a grove of the largest living things on earth and have them all to ourselves!"

Morgan said, "This area makes me feel like we've gone back to dinosaur times."

Then James recalled some of the information posted at the trailhead about Redwood Canyon. "This is the largest remaining sequoia grove in the world!"

"Converse Basin used to be," Morgan added.

"Used to be," Dad echoed. "Before almost all of those trees were cut down."

The Parkers fell silent, walking into the heart of the grove. There were glimpses of and close encounters with the gigantic, reddish barked trees. Soon though, they heard the gurgling of Redwood Creek. Eventually, down the trail from the main junction, the family found a perfect camping area, a flat spot not too far from the creek that had been used by backpackers before them.

The family began to settle in. Morgan helped

James put up the tent, inflated air mattresses, and spread out the sleeping bags. Dad found a place away from camp to cook. Mom and Dad took two of their bear-resistant food canisters to the cooking area and stashed one a good distance away. Then Dad set up the camp stove while Mom filtered water in the creek. Finally, the family gathered to cook and eat dinner.

While enjoying their well-earned meal, the Parkers sat in the shade of the dense, giant forest. Because of all the large trees, evening came early that night to the family and it was pleasantly cool. Their stew was savory and hot, and like all meals cooked outdoors, it tasted better than what they would have eaten at home.

As she ate her stew, Morgan daydreamed about what it would have been like to be at Converse Basin, once the largest sequoia grove in the world, during its heyday. . . .

It was the late 1800s and Morgan and James were watching the lumber crew in the busy grove of massive trees.

It was a very chaotic and noisy scene in Converse Basin. In one area, a group of workers had dug out a ditch about ten feet wide for a huge tree to fall into. Inside the ditch were hundreds of small branches, piled up as a sort of pillow for the sequoia to land on. Nearby, two workers were standing on a wooden scaffold propped up against the base of one of the giant trees that was still standing. They were vigorously hacking away with axes into the tree. The men had already chopped a gaping, triangular wedge into the tree, with a large pile of splintered wood debris below. But to Morgan, it appeared they still had a long way to go. One of the workers stopped to wipe the sweat off his forehead.

Cutting down Mark Twain Tree

"We've been at this thing for seven whole days now," he said. "It should come down at any time."

Morgan whispered to James as they watched the proceedings. "I think they dug up that big hole over there and filled it with branches and twigs so that the tree doesn't fall apart when it hits the ground. Sequoias, for being so big, are actually really fragile."

James surveyed the area below the tree, presumably where it was going to fall. "A lot of times they did that," he recalled. "Because if it just falls onto dirt and rock, the tree shatters, not leaving much wood that can be used. I heard they call that ditch a featherbed."

One of the workers on the scaffolding suddenly called out, "There she goes!"

Everyone in the vicinity immediately dashed as far away as possible from where they expected the giant sequoia to come crashing down.

The tree creaked and cracked, tipping slowly at first, then it gained momentum as it sped toward the ground and finally slammed onto its bed of branches.

When the tree landed, it kicked up a cloud of debris. It see-sawed a little, and then settled again, all in one piece.

Once the tree was still, Morgan said to James, "That tree sure came down quickly. I thought they'd have to cut it for hours more."

The twins struggled with mixed feelings. It was incredibly exciting to witness the loggers skillfully fell one of the world's largest trees first-hand, but it was also sad. These giants might be gone forever, considering the pace of the logging crew, and perhaps never be replaced.

James and Morgan scanned the area. They saw a mill building where the sequoias were sawn into lumber. There was also a large water tank with hoses, ladders, and buckets nearby. Other buildings included a store, cookhouse, blacksmith shop, and houses for the workers. Hundreds of men were busy, moving around the basin doing their work of the day. The twins also saw several sequoias that had been cut into sections. One man was measuring a section of a sequoia using a thick piece of string as a ruler. On top of a nearby hill was a small railroad locomotive and a large carrier behind

it stacked with sequoia lumber. The small train was carrying the wood up a steep ridge to the other side of the hill where the wood was then dumped into Sequoia Lake. There, men guided stacks of wood into a flume for a ride down to the valley.

Then Morgan noticed one huge sequoia up on a hill from where they were, un-cut and standing all by itself, towering over the basin. "I guess they left that tree alone," she pointed out to James.

"It's the Boole Tree," one of the workers nearby said. "We left that one unlogged in honor of our manager Frank Boole. It's the tallest tree around here as far as I can see. I would guess over 250 feet high. It's also one of the widest sequoias I have ever seen any-where. Something has to be left to show the world how impressive these trees really are!"

In the late 1800s, cutting down a sequoia was only the first of a logger's challenges. An equally large problem loomed: how to get the lumber to market. Sequoias grow high on the western slope of the rugged Sierra Nevada, far from big towns. Narrow, twisting canyons and steep slopes made road and railroad construction expensive and impractical. Instead, the logging companies built flumes—wooden channels filled with water—that snaked along hillsides and down valleys. Timber loaded into a flume could float many miles down to mills in the lowlands. The flume from Converse Basin to the town of Sanger was fifty-four miles long!

3

"There's a bear in camp!" Mom called out.

Morgan jumped up. "Where?"

"Over there," Mom said, pointing toward the edge of the clearing.

The bear was cinnamon colored. It looked fairly large, nearly a full-sized adult. The Parkers watched it pawing away at a downed log about thirty feet from camp. The bear tore apart the end of the log, sending splinters of wood scattering to the forest floor. Then it licked up some insects that it had exposed by ripping apart the tree.

"I was wondering, before, why that log was so shredded," Dad said.

"What kind of bugs do you think are in there?" James asked.

"Ants, termites, beetles. I imagine it eats them all," Mom said. "They are a great source of protein for the bear."

The Parkers watched the bear, mesmerized by its antics.

"It kind of feels like we're watching a nature show," James said. "It's so close."

The bear stopped eating. It lifted its head and looked at the Parkers. Right about then the family realized much of their food was nearby, strewn about with pots, pans, dishes, and leftovers—all outside of the bear-resistant canister.

Morgan looked at everything scattered around. She recalled from a ranger talk that bears don't see that well but their sense of smell is about twenty times better than a dog's. Morgan spoke slowly to her family. "What should we do with all this?" she said, gesturing to their meal.

Mom and Dad immediately started gathering everything as close as possible. "Hey Bear!" Dad said. "Don't worry about us. We're just cleaning up after dinner."

The bear took another look at the family then turned away to forage more in the forest.

Morgan, James, Mom, and Dad let out a sigh of relief. "Perfect behavior, bear!" Mom praised. "You go on eating your food and we'll clean up ours."

The Parkers hurriedly stuffed

Bear-resistant food canisters are required in many national park and wilderness areas in the West, and wherever bears dwell. Backcountry rangers inspect all wilderness camper's gear to make sure canisters are being used properly. Overnight hikers in the wilderness without one may be fined, have their food removed, or they can even be evicted from the wilderness. To be effective, a canister must be completely resistant to a bear's incredible strength and intelligence. They also must be too large for a bear to be able to carry away. To become approved, a trial canister with food in it is placed for field tests with live bears in zoos or other facilities. Above all, the canister must thwart a bear's best efforts to open it. Bears don't have opposable thumbs like humans, but they can be nimble with their claws and are very good problem solvers. Most canisters are designed to be opened only with some sort of tool, like a small screw driver. In the wilderness, canisters should be placed on the ground so bears don't drop them and potentially break them. They should also be wedged between rocks so they can't be rolled away.

everything away into the open bear canister. "We can clean the plates, pots, and spoons when we get back to civilization tomorrow," Dad said.

In the midst of the family's scrambling, the bear continued to search nearby for its own food. That's when James noticed it turn and walk toward their other, closed bear canister stashed about fifty feet away.

"Look!" James called out.

Whether the bear could smell the food or was just curious, it was impossible to tell. But the bear walked over to the canister, poked at it for a moment, then tipped it over and rolled it around. Then the bear pawed at the canister, trying to hold it down in an attempt to pry it open. But its rounded shape proved impossible for the bear. It soon gave up and padded off into the forest, taking one more glance at the Parkers along the way.

"Next time we'll need to wedge it between some rocks so a bear can't move it around like that," Dad said.

Once the bruin was completely out of sight, Mom said, "You know they field test those things. And I guess that's a good thing."

"Our canister passed the test," Dad added.

The family quickly finished cleaning and packing. Then they ran over and grabbed the canister that the bear had moved around. Morgan rolled the canister around looking for scratches or punc-tures, but didn't notice any.

They searched the area and put their containers in a new spot, properly wedged between rocks.

Soon it was almost dark and everyone gathered near the tent. Once the family was inside they fell asleep to the sounds of the night: crickets, an owl hooting, and the small stream gurgling along. But they never saw or heard the bear again. Keeping a clean camp gave the bear no reason to return.

When Morgan awoke the next morning, she saw streams of sunlight slanting through the forest. Morgan quietly climbed out of the tent, sat down on a nearby log, and gazed in awe at her surroundings—early morning, amidst a forest of giant trees. Alone, with her family soundly asleep, Morgan's thoughts drifted back again to a time long ago....

Morgan and James spoke to a gathering of curious but skeptical onlookers. "It took Morgan and me eleven days using saws, axes, and mauls to cut down this giant. We call it the 'California Tree.' We then split it into sections to haul back East and display here for the nation to see."

"I don't believe any of this," someone in the audience called out.

Despite the doubt brewing among the crowd, James spoke on more earnestly. "I was skeptical when I first saw these trees, too. But there are hundreds, maybe thousands more growing in California's Sierra Nevada. This tree and others like it are very real!"

"The California Tree," someone said sarcastically, "It sounds more like the 'California Hoax.' No trees could be this big. I don't know exactly what you have here. But it certainly couldn't have been one real, living tree."

James tried his best to convince the crowd. "We wanted to show it to you so you would know about them, too. I was amazed when I first saw them. I thought there is nothing living in the world that is this big! But, I promise you, they are all very, very real."

Morgan spoke up. "We must preserve these giant trees," she said to the increasingly annoyed crowd. "Before they all get cut down. That's why I'm proposing the area where they live be set aside as a national park, just like Yellowstone."

"Nothing in the world quite like this," Mom said.

Morgan jumped up, not realizing she was no longer alone in her thoughts of the past. She took a deep breath. "You can say that again," she agreed.

Soon the rest of the Parkers piled out of the tent.

Moving slowly at first, reveling in their surroundings, the Parkers grabbed a quick snack as they packed up camp, planning to enjoy a bigger meal once they returned to their car at the trailhead in a few hours.

4

After their backpack adventure in Redwood Canyon, the Parkers enjoyed a "rest day" at Dorst Creek Campground on the General's Highway. They set up their tent, read books, watched deer down by the creek, and roasted marshmallows after dinner.

The next day, they stopped at the Little Baldy trailhead. After a steady climb on long, easy switchbacks, the Parkers left the forested area behind and came to the top of a bare granite dome named Little Baldy. From the flatter top of this grand summit, the family took in a view of mountains and ridges in every direction.

"Hey, look at this!" James said, ignoring the view and looking down at his feet.

A small, round, metal plaque was embedded in the rock. It noted the dome's elevation at the top of Little Baldy at 8,044 feet.

"We are way up there now," Mom said. "But, still, well over 6,000 feet lower than where we'll be on the summit of Mount Whitney."

The family took in more of their surroundings. Far off to the west were the foothills and, beyond that, the San Joaquin Valley shrouded in summer heat and smog. Closer in was Redwood Canyon, where they had recently backpacked. "There are the round-topped sequoias we camped under last night," James pointed out.

"I wonder where that bear is now," Morgan said. "I hope it's eating more insects."

"Or sleeping after a hearty, natural meal," Mom added.

The family scanned the horizon some more. To the south was the Lodgepole area and the most famous of all sequoia groves, the Giant Forest. "We'll be there soon enough," Mom said. "And while we're there, we can go see the largest tree in the world."

Far above the Giant Forest were the Castle Rocks, penetrating the horizon. And just barely sticking out from the sequoias in the Giant Forest was the "thumb" of a massive granite dome. "I believe that is Moro Rock down there," Dad pointed out.

"We're going to climb that, right?" James asked.

"Very soon," Dad responded.

Despite all that they'd seen so far from the summit of Little Baldy, the best views were to the east. The backbone of the Sierra was there, with its series of sculpted pinnacles and spire-shaped mountains. Most of their tops were completely barren and all were at least 10,000 feet above sea level, with some much higher.

"Those mountains are amazing," Dad said in awe.

"But they are so dry now," Mom replied. "Usually you can see at least some snow on them this time of year. The extended drought has taken its toll."

"I see a snow patch up there!" Morgan exclaimed. The tiny, white spot was perched just below one of the park's highest peaks.

"There's another one!" James pointed out. "That one is really small though. I can barely see it."

Mom and Dad tried to name some of the mountains using the park map. "There's the Palisades, I think," Dad said. "On the east side of those peaks remains the largest glacier in the Sierra."

"I think that one is likely Mount Brewer," Mom said, looking directly east.

"Can we see Mount Whitney from here?" James asked, hoping to glimpse the peak they would be climbing in just a few days.

"I don't think so," Mom replied. "It has a distinct look and I am sure I would recognize it. I think it's behind those peaks just to the southwest."

Dad looked further south. "Back there somewhere is the Mineral King area," he mentioned.

"Mineral King?" Morgan asked.

"Oh—only one of my favorite places ever," Dad replied. "I spent quite a bit of time there while I was in college. It's a wonderful high-mountain valley surrounded by tall peaks of granite and high-elevation lakes. It's a hiker's and backpacker's dream with streams, waterfalls, plenty of wildlife, and even a couple of giant sequoia groves. But few people go there because of the incredibly long and winding road up."

"Are we going to go there?" James asked.

"If we have time," Mom replied.

Then Dad added, "As beautiful and wild as Mineral King is, it almost didn't end up that way."

So, while perched on top of Little Baldy, Dad told the family what he knew about the history of Mineral King and how it was almost turned into a humongous ski resort.

"As I understand, the Mineral King Valley was first inhabited by the Yokut Tribe of Native Americans." Dad began to tell what he knew of the hidden gem of Sequoia National Park. "The floor of the valley is at 7,400 feet, so they came up to Mineral King in summer and spent winters at lower elevations. But in the 1870s, prospectors found silver in the mountains surrounding the valley. Miners built the first road into the valley in 1873. Today, a twenty-five-mile, winding, twisting paved highway runs along the East Fork of the Kaweah River into the upper basin. Silver mining continued in Mineral King until the early 1900s, but mining there was too expensive to keep going, so it was pretty much abandoned. Later, in the 1930s and '40s, the area's beauty was recognized and people built resort cabins up there. Some of those summer homes are still in Mineral King today. But Mineral King's final chapter of history, at least as far as I know, started in the 1960s when the Disney Corporation tried to turn the whole Mineral King basin into a major ski resort. It was rumored that even Walt Disney himself was interested in skiing there."

As Dad shared more details of the history of Mineral King, James again turned back the clock, this time, instantly using what Dad was telling him. In James's mind, he and Morgan stood in pristine Mineral King Valley with the high peaks and tumbling cascades behind them. James was giving a speech about preserving the area.

"Fellow citizens and esteemed members of Congress," James spoke to a dignified crowd of politicians and others gathered. "I want to share with you why this very special place desperately needs your protection."

The well-dressed and important group of people gazed up at this nearly ten-year-old boy, obviously speaking well beyond his age, so poised and passionate as he shared his plea.

"This is a deep glacial valley just outside the border of Sequoia National Park—one of our first and original national parks. Well, this very special place, as you can see, has beautiful lakes, plunging streams, and giant sequoia groves all its own. Native Americans once lived here and silver was discovered in the area in the 1870s. An access road was built to get to Mineral King, but then, because they couldn't make enough money, the miners left."

James paused for a second then turned toward Morgan. "I think it's your turn now," he said.

Morgan cleared her throat and continued. "Now we all love Disneyland, right? But the Disney Corporation wants to build an immense ski resort right here in the heart of Mineral King. It will have up to twenty-seven ski lifts, giant parking lots, and," Morgan glanced at her prepared notes wanting to get all the details right for this critical part of the speech, "serve up to 2 million skiers a year. That, I guess, will be great for skiers and fine for the Disney Company. But what about the rest of us? What about the giant sequoias and the incredible scenery? What about the bears, wolverines, pikas, hawks, pine martens, and other very special creatures that call this place home?" Morgan paused for emphasis. "I think we should preserve and protect Mineral King area as part of Sequoia National Park for future generations."

Some in the audience clapped for the speech given by the twins. Others whispered among themselves, appearing not to be convinced of the need to designate the area for protection. Some wanted Disney to develop the resort and respectfully felt differently than Morgan and James.

In James's daydream, he looked toward Morgan, gesturing, what do we do now?

"Maybe answer questions from the audience?" Morgan replied. And they were about to when. . . .

A powerful gust of wind ripped James's hat right off his head. He snapped out of his imaginary speech and pounced on the hat before it blew straight off Little Baldy Dome. James stood up and put his hat tightly down on his head.

Then James looked at Dad. "What happened to Mineral King in the end?" he asked.

"The Sierra Club and other conservation groups in the 1960s fought to protect it. And they won. In 1978, the whole area was added to Sequoia National Park."

"That's a relief," James said, wondering how he might have ended his and Morgan's speech, and whether it would have made a difference. "I am so glad."

5

Eager to do more hikes, the Parkers decided to trek to a waterfall in Kings Canyon National Park. They drove north on a winding road, past the campgrounds at Cedar Grove to a trailhead at Roads End. The area near the ranger kiosk was teeming with hikers and backpackers. Some were filling up water bottles

at the spigot in front of the small building. Others were making their final plans and picking up bear canisters, supplies, maps, and permits for their long treks into the wilderness."Over there," Mom said, pointing toward the edge of the clearing.

Mom commented, noticing all the people with backpacks, "I can see where this hike's going to lead us."

"Wanting more?" James asked.

"Exactly," Mom replied.

The first few miles on the Mist Falls Trail were flat and easy, in mostly open terrain. Ponderosa pines and oaks were scattered about, but the trail was mostly bathed in warm sunshine and the river was far off and unseen.

A little over two and a half miles into the walk, the Parkers came to a junction and turned east. The trail climbed up and along granite boulders and stairs cut into the rock. The river now paralleled the trail, and the sound of rushing water and cascading currents accompanied the family on the trek to the popular waterfall.

Many other people were also on the hike. "It's a little pilgrimage, this route," Dad said in between guzzling down some freshly filtered, ice-cold water. Then Dad commented, "This is so refreshing! It must melt right off the snowfields higher up, where we'll be in a few days!"

The family hiked on. As they did, the views beckoned them further. The sheer-walled, U-shaped canyon they were in most certainly was glaciated and reminded the Parkers of a very popular national park neighbor to the north, Yosemite, an area also known for glaciated, granite scenery.

Eventually Morgan, James, Mom, and Dad came to a sign next to the trail announcing "Mist Falls." But the sign was not needed. The falls were living up to their name as mist was wafting in the air far away from the falls, cooling the Parkers and other people milling about. Powerful Mist Falls itself cascaded down Woods Creek in a torrent, sending up a loud roar.

The Parkers took in their surroundings. The vivid blue skies contrasted exquisitely with large, gray and white granite boulders, the tumbling and cascading falls, and the misty air surrounding them. Other hikers waded in the water holes below the falls, while some only dipped

in their toes. Just away from the stream was a dense forest. The whole area was quite picturesque. Mom said, "I think we're going to have our picnic lunch in a postcard!"

And that's what the family did. They quickly found a nice place to sit and eat and enjoy the view. It was a well-deserved lunch, especially after the almost five-mile hike. For the next hour or so, the family ate, sun-bathed, filtered and drank a lot of ice-cold Sierra snowmelt water, waded and splashed in small plunge pools, and eventually dozed off by the stream below Mist Falls.

Sometime later Dad woke up and sat upright. He saw Mom reading and Morgan and James dangling their feet into a small, clear, calm pool of water nearby.

"How long was I out?" Dad asked.

"About half an hour," Morgan replied.

"I couldn't help it," Dad responded. "The whole scene here has me mesmerized. It's like I'm in a trance, especially with the warm sun on these cool rocks." Dad paused and reflected a moment trying to think of exactly the right words to describe his feelings.

"I guess the whole area's like a natural white noise machine. I could sleep on the rocks by the creek here like a baby! And there's the cool water and warm sun and everything."

"I guess, then, at some point on this trip, or another in the future, we're going to have to go on and hike farther into the backcountry," Mom said, noticing the continual stream of backpackers a short distance off on the trail trekking to and from the high country.

Then Mom remembered. "The Rae Lakes Loop is up this way. I hiked that in college and there's more beyond that. From what I remember it was some of the finest

backcountry scenery anywhere. Sequoia and Kings Canyon are a backpacker's paradise!"

"Do you think that James and I could do the Rae Lakes hike?" Morgan asked.

"It is quite a journey," Mom said, while thinking. "As I recall, it's over forty miles, with quite a bit of climbing. But if we took our time, I am sure you could do it," Mom said. "And you would love it!"

"Maybe that will be our next hiking trip here after we climb Mount Whitney," Dad mused.

James noticed his family all staring downstream from Mist Falls. A large black bear was walking right across a log from one side of the stream to the other. The bear lumbered along, moving gracefully across the thin log without any care to issues of balance.

"I wish I could do that so easily," Mom said.

Once the bear reached the other side, it stepped off the log and ambled into the forest.

"Cool!" James said.

Eventually the Parkers left Mist Falls behind. Soon the roar of the crashing waterfall was too far off to hear. They went down the same trail they had come up. By late afternoon they were back at Roads End.

The family ended the day walking along the wooden walkway at Zumwalt Meadows. The path led them to two benches overlooking the heart of the meadow with towering granite cliffs above. They spent some quiet time there, soaking it all in. Then they drove to Cedar Grove and Moraine Campground for the night.

6

The Parkers drove into the Lodgepole area early in the morning, having reserved a campsite in this very popular part of the park in advance. They passed the visitor center and store parking lots. Soon they were at the kiosk of the campground entrance station. A posted sign warned about bear activity in the area. "Three vehicle break-ins in the last seven days," it read.

"We know where all our food is going as soon as we park the car," James said.

"And anything else that has a scent," Morgan added. "It will all go in the bear lockers."

The family found their campsite, quickly set up, and then walked over to the Tokopah Falls Trail, right out of camp.

The busy trail climbed gently through the forest. The small Kaweah River cascaded and plunged into crystal clear pools of water alongside the trail. Many particularly inviting pools were already taken by visitors spending the late morning there swimming, wading, and playing in or near the water.

"I know where we're going later today!" James announced, noticing at least one deep, clear pool not yet full of people.

"It's going to be awfully cold!" Dad laughed.

The family hiked on, soon leaving the large campground behind. After crossing a small footbridge over a side stream, the Parkers realized they hadn't seen anyone on the trail for some time. They were all alone.

Thinking of the bears they saw in Redwood Canyon and Mist Falls, and the warning at the campground entrance station, Morgan suddenly sang out, "Hey oh!"

"Hey oh!" Dad echoed.

Other than the family's loud and repeated warning calls, the morning was quiet. No large omnivores made any appearances.

What the Parkers did get to see though, was at least equally impressive. Tokopah Valley was a large, glacially sculpted, U-shaped valley. A massive, ice-scoured cliff rose above the south side of the valley. Called the Watchtower, it towered far above the Parkers and cast a giant morning shadow across the trail. On the valley floor were forested meadows and the headwaters of the Kaweah River.

Soon the Parkers came to an area with large boulders. As James led the way he saw a tiny rabbit-like animal dash into a little crack between the rocks, hiding from the much larger human creatures that had just invaded its territory. "Hey, what was that?" James called out.

Then the family heard a short, high-pitched whistle. Another little fur ball was perched on a boulder nearby. James noticed that one too. "That's what I saw a minute ago down there," James exclaimed.

The tiny animal twitched its nose and watched the family hike by. Then, suddenly, as the trail edged closer to the animal, it too dashed into a mini cave and was out of sight.

Mom knew right away what it was. "It's a pika,"

she informed everyone. "They live in very cold, isolated, high-elevation areas. So, I guess that says something about winters and the overall climate here in Tokopah Valley. Their fur is too thick for warm places. They just get too hot."

The family trekked on and soon reached the end of the trail. Tokopah Falls plunged down from the cliffs above, dropping into pools of water.

The Parkers took in the whole scene— the waterfall, clear pools of water, gigantic boulders, the meadows, and the towering Watchtower.

"It's pretty awesome in here isn't it?" Dad said.

Morgan nodded her head in agreement then took a swig of water.

Morgan, James, Mom, and Dad were just outside of the Giant Forest. They hiked along cliff edges with sheer drop-offs, using the rails and over 350 stairs and steps to climb Moro Rock. Despite the persistent crowd all the way up the granite dome, the Parkers arrived at the top in a little over twenty minutes. The trail topped out along a peninsula of rock with railings on both sides. The views from that vantage point were incredible.

First the Parkers gazed west and were once again greeted with haze and smog. "The valley is out there somewhere," Mom said.

James looked below the massive rock they were

standing on, noticing the twisting and turning highway in the much less forested foothills. He saw all the cars making the slow, curvy drive into the park. "Are we going to be on that road?" James asked.

"On our way out of here and back home," Dad replied.

Far below the end of the dome was the Kaweah River Canyon. "There's got to be water down there somewhere," Dad said.

"But it's sure a long way down!" James responded.

"I think nearly 3,000 feet," Mom added.

East of the Kaweah River Canyon they could see the tall peaks, known as the backbone of the Sierra Nevada. Rock bound and above tree line at the top, the peaks were nearly barren of snow. It was similar to the view that they enjoyed on Little Baldy.

Morgan turned back toward the direction they'd come from. She immediately noticed the distinct rounded tops of sequoia trees. "There's the Giant Forest!" she called out.

And sure enough, from the top of Moro Rock there appeared to be hundreds of large sequoias below, not very far away.

The family spent some more time perched on their magnificent natural platform. Then they scampered down the same trail they had come up, meeting a steady stream of hikers headed up to the top of Moro Rock. At one point, the family had to scoot sideways to let the hikers

Sequoia and Kings Canyon National Parks are a paradise of big trees, canyons, waterfalls, and high mountains. But some people have called the twin parks a "polluted paradise." These two national parks are the smoggiest in the country. The problem comes from the San Joaquin Valley below. That mostly rural, farming area has worse air than just about any large city in the United States. The causes are many, including: extremely busy freeways with a lot of trucks, freight train traffic, dairy cow farms, food processing plants, and incredibly high amounts of diesel tractor use. In addition, the polluted air at the southern end of the valley gets trapped by the surrounding mountains and the region's consistently stagnant weather patterns. Studies have been conducted on the giant sequoias at both parks. Many conifers are hurt by the pollution, but, so far the giant trees seem to be holding their own. However, if sequoia saplings are exposed to high levels of smog, many of them become stunted. There are movements to clean the air at both parks. One of them is the shuttle bus system that carries visitors to the parks and popular destinations within each park.

go by. Morgan whispered to James. "Were we breathing that hard on the way up?"

"I think so," James replied. "It's a lot easier going down."

At the bottom of the dome, the family caught the free shuttle bus to the Giant Forest Museum.

Once they arrived at the museum, the Parkers walked among the displays.

There they learned that the Giant Forest is one of the largest remaining sequoia groves, with more than 2,000 large, mature trees. They also read about other groves of sequoias in and around the park. And that some of the trees are up to 3,000 years old.

"Well, they may be the most massive trees in the world as far as volume, but they aren't the tallest," Dad pointed out. "It says here that some redwoods can grow to 370 feet high!"

"I just found out another secret to the sequoia," James announced. "Each tree puts out thousands of cones and tons of small seeds. But only a very few grow to become giants."

Morgan shared another fact. "Did you know that it takes 91,000 sequoia seeds to make one pound? Each seed is about the size of a flake of oatmeal."

"They're that small," Mom said in awe. "And yet they make a tree so large."

The family's last few minutes at the museum were spent playing a game, "Wheel of Fortune," which demonstrated the possible plight of a single sequoia seed.

James spun the large wheel first. The arrow landed on "Forest litter too deep. Sprout can't reach soil."

Morgan spun next and read out loud the same result.

Mom went next. Her spin stopped on, "Not enough rain. Seedling dries out. I guess that seed came out of a cone during a drought," Mom said.

Then it was Dad's turn. His spin led to "Seed lands in a bad spot and never sprouts."

After they all took several more turns with no luck for any of their supposed sequoia seeds, James took matters in his own hands. He manually turned the wheel until the arrow pointed on, "Mature tree. Good chance of growing real big."

A ranger was wandering in the museum. She came by and watched James put the arrow on the one small spot for success and said, "The chances of becoming a big, mature sequoia tree are actually a lot less than that."

"What are the chances?" Morgan asked.

"Oh, somewhere around one in a million," the ranger said, then smiled. "The secret of the sequoia is to put out a lot of seeds. The few lucky, well-placed ones will become the giant sequoias of the future."

"We've been talking about sequoia secrets all week," James said.

"Like good soil, plenty of sunlight, and enough—but not too much— moisture," Mom responded.

"Exactly," Morgan replied.

"You all sure know your sequoias," the ranger said, smiling. Then she wandered off to chat with other visitors. James spun the wheel again to test their sequoia seed's luck one more time. "Forest litter too deep. Sprout can't reach the soil" is what he got again. "Oh, well," James said. "Better luck next time!"

Outside they caught the bus to Lodgepole and walked back to camp.

8

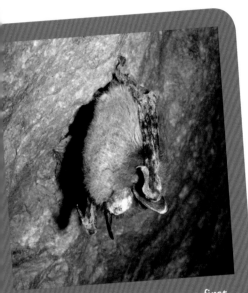

White-Nose Syndrome was first discovered in New York state in 2007. Since then, the fungus has spread across the eastern United States and Canada, killing millions of bats. At Sequoia National Park, scientists and park managers are working to protect the bats that live in Crystal Cave. The spider-web gate at the cave's entrance lets bats pass through, but it keeps out people who might try to sneak in instead of taking one of the tours. And visitors on cave tours must walk on a disinfectant mat before entering the cave to make sure no fungus spores are on their shoes.

After a long and winding, scenic drive down into the foothills below the Giant Forest, the Parkers came to the Crystal Cave parking area. At the kiosk they checked in with their group for the 10 A.M. tour.

At the top of a trail leading down to the cave, a guide asked the Parkers to step on a mat coated with disinfectant. The guide explained, "Many bats in caves across the country are being exposed to a disease that causes them to grow a white fungus under their nose and other body parts. The disease is called White-Nose Syndrome. It causes bats to come out of hibernation when they shouldn't and use up too much energy. Sometimes they fly during the day and hunt for insects that aren't there. This is killing bats in many places, which is also causing the local bug populations to jump. The disease is sometimes carried by people walking on infected areas. We don't want that to happen here at Crystal Cave. That is why we require all who enter Crystal Cave to step on this mat, which has been treated to kill the disease."

Dad walked over the mat first. "Well, that's a first," he commented, "But I am glad to do my part."

Then the family began a half-mile trek down into a thick, oak-laden forest with a cascading waterfall. "This part of the park reminds me of Great Smoky Mountains National Park back east," Mom said, referring to the large variety of trees in the dense forest along the trail.

Soon they came to the cave entrance area where their Crystal Cave tour guide greeted the Parkers and all the others who bought tickets for the tour.

Once she introduced herself and explained how the cave tour would proceed, the guide said to the group, "Please don't touch anything in the cave. This is an essential rule for going underground. Natural oils on your skin can damage any cave formation."

Then, after going over the rest of the rules for the underground adventure, the guide led everyone to a thick metal spider web that blocked the cave's entrance.

"Anyone want to climb through the web?" the guide joked, knowing there wasn't a single person who could fit. But then she added, "The giant web was built by the Civilian Conservation Corp in the 1930s. But don't worry, we won't get caught in it."

The guide unlocked a door on the web and pushed a part of it open, making for a normal sized doorway.

The guide began the tour by saying, "There are over 200 caves in Sequoia and

Kings Canyon National Parks. But the one you just entered, Crystal Cave, is the only one open to the public."

The group passed through the cave's twilight zone—the last part of the cave to still receive some natural daylight. Quickly the cool underground air enveloped the visitors. The guide turned on electric lights positioned throughout the cave and the adventure was on.

Right away the group passed two gloved volunteers just off the trail who appeared to be cleaning parts of the cave. "Don't mind us," one called out while looking at the stream of visitors passing by.

The Parkers though, slowed down to watch. One of the workers shared, "This is actually my summer job, cleaning lint in the cave." The worker held up two of her tools for the job. "And these are what I use more than anything else, a paintbrush and tweezers."

That grabbed Morgan's and her family's attention. "What exactly do you do?" Morgan asked.

The worker replied, "I find lint all over cave walls. The lint is from the visitors who have walked on the exact path you are on now. Lint comes from fibers from people's clothes, hair, and even dead skin cells." The worker looked at the walls of the cave. "Lint gets on these cave walls and discolors them or stops their natural growth. Cave formations are always growing you know, even if it's so slow we can't see it."

"Anyway," the worker finished, "Our job here is to clean the cave and restore it to its natural condition." She smiled at the Parkers then gestured up toward the group, now far ahead. "You better go catch up with them!" she said playfully.

The Parkers left the clean-up crew behind and hurried to rejoin the tour.

Soon after, the group passed an underground creek cascading through a polished marble chute.

Deeper underground they went. The guide pointed out the many spectacular cave formations along the way, including cave coral, flowstone, stalactites, stalagmites, and cave popcorn.

At one point the guide said, "Crystal Cave was discovered in 1918. So it is just about to have its 100th birthday. Is anyone here with us that old?"

Everyone laughed.

"The cave we are in is actually about 1.2 million years old," the guide said. "So it isn't really the cave's 100th birthday. That's just its centennial that marks the start of human exploration. But water has been carving this series of underground passages a lot longer than that."

The Parkers and the whole group were led deeper into the cave.

"The formations sometimes look like giant pieces of Swiss cheese," James pointed out to his family.

"I think that thing looks like baleen from a whale," Morgan said as they scooted along.

"There's something, to me, that looks like an octopus's head and tentacles," Mom said.

The twins smiled and Morgan said, "I can totally see that!"

After a bend in the trail, James announced, "I can really see the crystals in the rocks up here!"

Then Morgan added, "And that whole area looks like layers of brain."

The guide had been listening to the Parkers talk about the features of the cave. "One's imagination can really go wild," she said, "when trying to describe cave for-mations. There really is nothing like this up on the Earth's surface. That's why early explorers wanted to protect Crystal Cave and open it up to groups like you. It's all about stewardship, keeping the cave—or anything in nature—in its natural state for future generations to enjoy."

The guide paused for a moment, letting everyone look around at the incredible formations. Then she explained, "Rainwater above mixes with carbon dioxide, a gas that occurs naturally. Kind of like the bubbles in soda pop. That helps dissolve rocks over millions of years into these formations. The carbon dioxide comes from plants and animals decaying in the soil. And that process is still going on today."

"By the way," the guide changed the subject, "we are not the only living creatures in here. There are some trogloxenes. These are creatures that sometimes visit caves but typically live outside. This includes bats, bears, skunks, and raccoons. Some of our caves also have troglophiles. These creatures can survive outside of a cave, but they prefer to be inside one. These include beetles, worms, and some species of frogs and salamanders, and sometimes crickets. They often stay inside caves their whole lives."

The guide paused a second, then continued, "Of course my favorite cave creature is called a troglobite, although they are not necessarily here in Crystal Cave. These creatures though can survive only in caves. They have poor or no eyesight, large antennas, and often are whitish because their skin has no pigment. This includes certain species of shrimp, fish, crayfish, millipedes, insects, and salamanders." The guide paused for a second then added, "Pretty interesting, huh?"

Finally, the guide led the group into the Marble Hall, the final room to see at Crystal Cave. Once everyone was situated in the large underground chamber, she warned everyone first, then turned off the lights.

The cave was completely black. Both Morgan and James held their hands in front of their faces.

"I can't even see my fingers," James reported.

"I can't see mine, either," Morgan whispered back.

The guide said, "This is the most unique part of the cave. Where else in the world can you see absolutely nothing?"

9

A shuttle bus brought the Parkers to a parking lot and trailhead. There, on a sign at an interpretive kiosk, was a quote from the famous conservationist and explorer, John Muir: "This part of the sequoia belt seemed to be the finest." The Parkers were about to find out why.

The family walked down a paved path with scores of other visitors. It wasn't long before they were able to look down at the world's largest tree. "There's the General Sherman!" Morgan exclaimed.

At a display near the giant tree, the family learned that the General Sherman is 109 feet around at its base. And it keeps getting bigger every year.

"It must've grown in just the perfect spot," James said as the family continued on toward the tree.

Soon Morgan, James, Mom, and Dad were at the base of the world's most massive sequoia. Swarms of other visitors were there, too, marveling at such an enormous living thing. Many people were lining up to take a picture with the sign at the base, with the General Sherman right behind them.

A plaque there gave more information about the tree.

Morgan worked her way in between the people and walked up to the sign. She summarized all that she could for her family who stood close by. "The General Sherman is the largest tree in the world by volume and weight. But the famous tree we saw earlier, the General Grant, is actually wider. Also, the General Sherman Tree is over 52,500 cubic feet in volume. If it were filled with water, there would be enough for one person to take a bath every day for twenty-seven years."

Morgan surprised her family when she told them that the General Sherman Tree is about 1,000 years younger than the oldest known sequoia. An older sequoia that once lived in Converse Basin survived until it was 3,266 years old.

GENERAL SHERMAN

Morgan also read that the General Sherman Tree weighs 1,395 tons and is 276 feet tall.

Soon, Ranger Colleen Bathe strolled up. "Hey, that's the ranger from the museum the other day," Morgan said.

The Parkers moved away from the sign and over to where Ranger Colleen stood in front of a gathered group.

Ranger Colleen smiled, acknowledging the Parkers by saying, "Well, we know this tree was clearly a winner in Sequoia Wheel of Fortune!"

The Parkers all laughed in response.

Then, after introducing herself to the crowd, Colleen gave a short talk about the General Sherman and sequoias.

"Welcome to the largest living thing in the world!" Colleen said. Then she joked, "No not me, the tree behind me." Colleen smiled and told the audience more.

"Believe it or not, that massive tree has very shallow roots. The roots go out about as wide as the tree is tall, but they only go down about one to one and a half meters deep. One of the secrets of the sequoia's survival," Colleen said, "is to have very shallow roots. The roots help the giant trees capture as much water as possible when rain or snow soaks the ground."

At this point the Parkers all looked at each other, acknowledging that everyone in the park seemed to be talking about the sequoia secrets to survival.

Colleen next held up a small, egg-shaped sequoia cone. "Here's another secret to their survival. Each tree drops hundreds of cones and thousands of seeds. Somewhere, hopefully, at least one will be successful and become a giant. Here, everyone, I am going to pass around one of their cones. And the clear vial also going around has one tiny sequoia seed in it. It's about the size of an oat flake."

Colleen passed the cone one way and the vial the opposite direction.

"Most seeds don't make it. Fungus or fire stops them from growing or even sprouting at all. Also, deer often browse on the saplings," Colleen continued.

"Baby sequoias are at the perfect height for deer. And that can lead to their demise. But, to become a giant sequoia resembling the General Sherman, conditions need to be perfect. A 'Sequoia Gargantuan,' as they are scientifically called, will need a large opening in the canopy for sunlight to get through. Such openings are often produced by a fire. Fire also releases nutrients to the soil, opens the cones, and cleans out the plant competition. And sequoias need well-watered soil."

"Obviously that's what happened with our good friend up here to make it to the size it is today," Colleen said.

The group took a moment to stare up at the giant sequoia towering above them.

Then Colleen went on, "The General Sherman Tree and all sequoia trees reach their full height at about 600 years. After that they keep growing wider but not taller."

A man who stood near Dad patted his stomach. "That kind of sounds like me," he said to his family.

Dad looked over at the man and smiled. "I said exactly that to my family the other day," he said.

Morgan looked up at her father. "Only you didn't take 600 years to get so tall," she quipped.

Colleen spoke again to the group. "The mid-Sierra elevation range is 5,500 to 7,500 feet. That's the wettest part of the mountains here and where almost all the sequoia groves are."

Colleen went on. "The Giant Forest is one such grove. It's one of the largest and perhaps the finest, as John Muir once said. But there are about seventy-five sequoia groves still alive in the central and southern Sierra Nevada."

"All are in California's Sierra Nevada, from south of here to west of Lake Tahoe."

Colleen finished her talk with enthusiasm. "Please take a walk here among the massive trees in our Giant Forest. We have forty miles of trails in the grove and they are all exceptionally beautiful."

The audience clapped and some stayed to ask the ranger questions.

10

The Parkers, meanwhile, decided to hike through the maze of paths that criss-crossed the Giant Forest, wanting to see more giant sequoias and to walk by some of the well-known and spectacular meadows along the way.

The family headed out on the Congress Trail toward Circle Meadow. Once they were beyond the General Sherman Tree, they realized they had left most of the people behind.

In the quiet of the trees, the Parkers meandered from point to point. They passed several junctions and turn-offs but few hikers. Along the way, they were in the cool shade of giant sequoias.

At one spot, Dad said, "I am just in awe of this forest. There are sequoias everywhere."

Soon they came to an abandoned wood shack named Cattle Cabin, nestled among the trees. The Parkers picnicked outside of the cabin, then moved on toward Circle and Huckleberry Meadows.

As the Parkers walked away from the cabin, Morgan said, "I wonder if they used to graze cattle out here somewhere. Maybe that's where it got its name."

"It would certainly have been an amazing place to live," Mom replied.

The family strolled along at a leisurely pace. However, as they approached Huckleberry Meadow, they all froze. Morgan pointed to the open grassy area and called out, "Hey! Look over there."

Right smack-dab in the middle of the meadow was an adult black bear, nibbling on the grass.

The rest of the family saw it, too. "Hey, bear!" Mom called out.

The bear didn't flinch or look up even though the Parkers were only about thirty feet away. It just kept on eating.

"Hey bear!" Mom repeated.

The California state flag has a grizzly on it, yet there are no longer grizzlies living in the state. Grizzly bears once thrived in California and it is estimated that up to 10,000 grizzly bears dwelled in the state. They were big bears, too, growing larger than the grizzlies that live in Montana and Wyoming today. California grizzly bears weighed around 600 pounds, some over 1,000 pounds. Their demise began when miners, who moved in for the Gold Rush in the mid-1800s, killed many grizzlies. Then, as ranchers moved in, the killing continued as bears were known to eat cattle. Some were even poisoned to death. By the 1900s, there were very few reports of any of the great bears left in the state. According to one account, the last California grizzly was shot near Sequoia National Park in 1922. Other reports indicate another grizzly roamed the Santa Barbara Mountains near the California coast and was last spotted in 1924. But none have been seen in the state since. There have been petitions to re-introduce grizzlies to California as some areas are considered suitable habitat, but so far this has not happened.

But the bear was busy foraging, paying no attention to the Parkers and their repeated calls.

"That's good," Mom said referring to the bear ignoring her family.

The family continued to watch the bear, only a short distance off the trail. "We should keep moving," Dad said. "We're awfully close to it standing right here."

As they walked away, Mom said, "That's an unusual color for a black bear. Sort of blondish, kind of like a grizzly bear. But I know grizzlies don't exist in California anymore."

The Parkers hiked on, passing large Crescent Meadow. Dad commented, "You gotta love these beautiful, lush meadows surrounded by giant trees. Where else do you get to see things like this?"

Mom replied by saying, "I think Sequoia National Park might be the only place."

The family's leisurely stroll continued. Soon they passed a pair of hikers going the opposite direction. Morgan decided to warn them about what was ahead. "There's a bear up ahead in Huckleberry Meadow."

The hikers stopped and smiled. One replied, "And there's a whole bunch more where you're heading!"

Morgan, James, Mom, and Dad all looked at each other, amazed and bewildered that there could be so many bears in such a small space. They wondered how many they would see next.

Soon the Parkers approached Log Meadow. The long, thin, grassy area was surrounded again by conifers, including plenty of giant sequoias. On the meadow's edge was a giant, downed sequoia named "Tharp's Log." The family stepped into an alcove at one end of the hollowed out tree.

Once inside, the family peered into the darkness that stretched out before them. As their eyes adjusted to the light they begin to make out the details. Mom looked around and realized, "It's a little home in here!"

The large, hollowed out log had many of the comforts of permanent living quarters: benches, shelves, a picnic table, a bedding area, a window, and even a place to build a fire with a chimney. Most of the essentials were made from parts of the inside of the downed tree. All of the wooden items were old, rustic, and broken apart. Clearly no one had lived in the log for a long time.

The family stepped outside of the makeshift home and into the light. They read that Hale Tharp, the caretaker of the meadow and the Giant Forest, spent many seasons out there, living in the log in the late 1800s.

While milling around, James imagined what life would be like back in the day and visiting Tharp's home. He let himself drift to a time and place where he and Morgan had just arrived to help Tharp and drop off some supplies. . . .

James and Morgan walked up to Tharp's Log in the heart of the Giant Forest. They noticed the freshly mortared rocks outside the cabin indicating where the fireplace was inside.

The twins greeted Tharp outside while he was clearing away some small branches that had fallen on and around his log home.

Morgan and James each hauled inside a large crate of supplies for Tharp. They unpacked them and put all the items on the table inside the log cabin for their friend to see. Then Morgan began to check the items that they had brought. "Let's see, we have rice, grains, hot cereal, oats, razors, coffee, beans, extra warm clothes and a blanket, toothpaste, soap, canned goods, fruits, and matches. That should be enough to get you through a few more weeks up here in the sequoia grove."

James also showed Tharp one more thing. He held up a book and said, "We brought you reading material, too."

"Thanks!" Tharp replied enthusiastically. "I really appreciate your efforts in re-stocking my shelves and keeping me going. As you know, it's a long way from the nearest town here in the Giant Forest. And it can take several days to get down and back up. So you bringing me all this really helps. But I wouldn't trade what I do for anything. Someone has to watch over the giant sequoias!"

THARP LOG

HALE D. THARP, PIONEER RESIDENT OF THE THREE RIVERS LOCALITY, FIRST VISITED GIANT FOREST IN 1858 ACCOMPANIED BY TWO YOKUTS INDIANS. HE LIVED IN THIS RUSTIC CABIN EACH SUMMER FROM 1861 UNTIL SEQUOIA NATIONAL PARK WAS ESTABLISHED IN 1890. HE USED THE NEARBY MEADOWS AS RANGE FOR HIS LIVE-STOCK.

THARP RECOGNIZED AS DISCOVERER OF GIANT FOREST. DIED AT HIS OLD THREE RIVERS RANCH HOME ON NOVEMBER 5, 1912 AT THE AGE OF 84 YEARS.

Then Tharp looked outside at the sun angling through the trees. He turned to the twins, "From the looks of things, you might consider getting yourselves going soon. You've got about thirty minutes or so until sunset."

But Morgan took a moment and looked around Tharp's home, noticing the open window and doorway. She asked with concern for Tharp's safety, "How do you keep the bears out?"

"It's not easy, and it requires constant vigilance," Tharp replied. "I do have that gun." Tharp pointed to a rifle mounted on one of the log's walls. "But I have never hurt a bear. I've shot bullets into the ground to scare a few away, though. But to be honest with you, with my cattle grazing out in the meadow here it probably makes many of the bears head to the next meadow over. I think bears like their meals a little quieter."

Tharp looked at all the food Morgan and James had brought. "As you know, a fed bear is a dead bear. And I need all my food. So I do everything I can to make sure they don't get to any of my stash. Much of it I keep under the bench here, and I weigh down the lid with rocks."

Tharp walked over to his makeshift fireplace and stove. He stoked the fire and rolled some wood around so it would burn on the other side. Then he reached over and stirred the stew heating inside a pot on the stove.

The hearty aroma from Tharp's cooking filled the hollow log's air. Instantly Morgan and James were hungry. Tharp picked up on that and offered his hospitality.

"Can I interest the two of you in some of my stew before you skedaddle on out of here? It's the least I can do after all you've done for me."

Although he didn't want to contribute to any reduction in Tharp's supplies, James' hunger was real. Still, trying to hold back, James walked over to the window cut out of the log and looked outside. There was no more sun shining through the trees in the forest. Nighttime was coming on fast. Still, James admitted, "I think the chill of the evening air is getting to me, along with the smell of food."

James turned to Tharp, and was about to give a thumbs up to the offer of a meal before he and Morgan had to go, but, a familiar voice interrupted his thoughts. . . .

"There's a bear out here!"

It was Dad calling out.

That snapped James out of his daydream. He and Morgan quickly dashed to the front of Tharp's Cabin and joined their parents at the edge of the meadow, making for a very tight-knit group of four.

The bear, like the one at Huckleberry Meadow, was in the middle of the large grassy area, directly across from the cabin. But that made it only about thirty feet away. It was a sub-adult—a younger bear—pawing at the ground and eating grass and flowers and whatever else was in the meadow.

"Hello, bear!" Morgan said to make sure the bear knew the Parkers were there.

Just like the ones they saw earlier, the bear ignored the Parkers and continued to forage.

Morgan, James, Mom, and Dad watched the bear for a moment or two and took some pictures. James said, "I wonder if this is one of the bears those people we saw earlier were talking about."

"What a beautiful home for the bears, and for Tharp," Mom said.

Soon the family left the bear and cabin behind and continued hiking along, circling Log Meadow. It wasn't long before the family got wind of another possible bear in the vicinity.

Up front, Mom warned her family of what was on the trail. "There's some awfully fresh bear scat up here!" she called out and stepped over a pile of droppings. The rest of the family following her did the same.

A moment later, James pointed and said. "There's a bear right up in that gully!"

The brown-colored bear was a short distance off the trail in a dry creek bed. Its ears were perked upright and it was staring right at the Parkers.

"I bet that's the one that just went to the bathroom," James declared.

The bear looked straight at the Parkers. Then it bobbed its head back and forth before pawing at the ground a moment. All that time, it stayed nearly in the same spot.

"It's acting a little skittish," Dad said. "I wonder if it wants to head back to the meadow and we're in its way."

The bear continued to glance around somewhat timidly, and as it did so it kept watching the Parkers and sniffing the air.

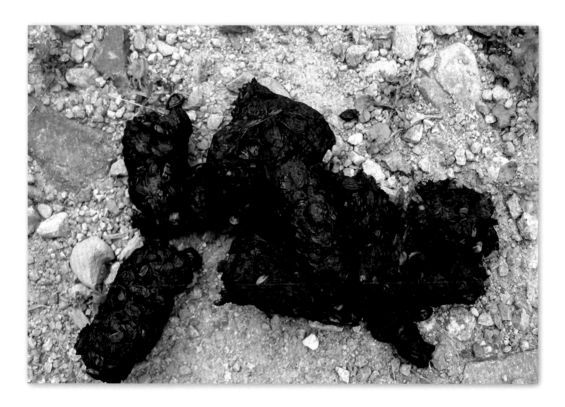

Mom said, "A nervous bear is not one that I particularly want us to hang around. Let's keep moving."

The family hiked on with Mom in the lead and Dad in the back. Morgan and James turned back several times to look for the bear and report on its status. Soon it was out of sight. A short time later the Parkers were directly across the meadow from Tharp's Cabin. Morgan stopped to take a picture of the lush, grassy area with the cabin on the other side. But, then, once again with a wide view of the meadow, the Parkers quickly spotted more omnivores.

"There are three more bears grazing in the meadow out that way," James exclaimed. "They're all pretty close to each other."

And, like all the bears the family had seen so far, none responded or seemed interested in the Parkers despite the family's persistent calls to warn them.

"I guess it's feeding time," Dad said. "I'm glad we came out here early enough to see them. And the bears are doing exactly what they should be doing, eating natural foods in a wild area. It's much more exciting than seeing bears in a zoo."

Giddy at all their bear sightings, the Parkers hiked on, now at full alert for what they might see next.

The trail continued to circle Log Meadow. Suddenly, Morgan called out, "Aw! How cute!"

There was another bear. This one though was curled up, sleeping on a log, perched out over the meadow. The bear stayed snug until the Parkers were about twenty feet away, still on the trail. The family paused for a second while Morgan took a picture of the sleeping, snug bear.

The bear heard the Parkers and opened its eyes. It looked up at them and yawned, then rolled over and closed its eyes again and tried to go back to sleep.

"C'mon," Mom said, ushering her family along. "You know how Dad and I are when we sleep in, we don't want to be disturbed, so let's give that resting bear some space."

As they walked briskly away from this latest bear sighting, James called out exuberantly, "It's bear city around here!"

"You can say that again," Dad said. "What a trail!"

"Say that again?" Morgan replied excitedly, "I will, because there's another bear up on that hill."

This one was up on a ridge walking across a slope above the family.

"Seven bears in or around one meadow!" Mom exclaimed. "You don't get to see that every day."

Then Mom thought for a moment before sharing. "I am just trying to figure why there are so many bears all in one place. I think, since many of them are sub-adults, maybe we are seeing bears from the same family. But there also must be a food source concentrated in these meadows that the bears know about and really like eating."

"I wonder what it is," Morgan replied.

As they got to the far end of the meadow, the family took one last glance back at the open, grassy area. Several of the bears were still visible. "Good-bye bears!" Morgan called out. "May you live a long, happy, and healthy life here in the Giant Forest!"

The Parkers were now headed toward the Crescent Meadow parking lot. Along the way they reported their animal sightings to hikers heading toward Log Meadow.

11

It was the middle of the night as Morgan and James and their parents trudged up the Mount Whitney Trail. The full moon cast an eerie light across the path as they hiked. Deep shadows filled the forest on either side of the trail. As the family hiked, all they could see were the rocks and dirt at their feet and the silhouette of the person in front. The only sounds were their boots scuffling along the trail.

The Parkers had spent the previous two days camped at Whitney Portal, 7,851 feet above sea level, to get used to the thinner air at high altitudes. Less oxygen makes breathing and hiking more difficult but now their bodies at least were somewhat more acclimated for their ascent up Mount Whitney, the tallest mountain in the United States outside of Alaska. Now it was just past three in the morning and each used their headlamps to light up a small circle of trail ahead of them, guiding their steps.

As the trail continued, the Parkers came to a stream crossing where they balanced on logs to reach the other side. As each of them made it across, he or she turned to shine their light for the next person, making sure no one slipped into the water. The family then hiked on, continuing their steady climb.

The trek was eleven miles from the trailhead to the top of the 14,494-foot mountain. The Parkers would hike a total of twenty-two miles and climb more than 6,500 feet (and come back down) all in one day. This was no gentle walk among the sequoias that they had done many times earlier in the week, or a stroll through the meadows of the Giant Forest.

This was a special hike. The other hikes that the Parkers had experienced in Sequoia and Kings Canyon National Parks during their annual summer vacation prepared them for this hike.

At almost three miles, the Parkers came to the junction with the Lone Pine Lake

Trail. It was still dark, so they decided to skip going to the lake, hoping they would have enough time and energy to see it later in the day on the way down.

The family remained mostly quiet. Talking was difficult anyway as they approached an altitude of 9,000 feet. Still, every once in a while someone in the family said something, interrupting the rhythmic sounds of footsteps on granite along with labored breathing.

"This just goes on and on," Morgan said, trying to glimpse what the trail ahead offered through the dim light of the moon.

"We'll have to stop again soon to filter water," James added after taking a gulp from his canteen.

"At least it's steady and not too steep of a pitch so far," Dad said.

"So far," Mom repeated.

Once again everyone stopped talking to save their energy. Their views continued of the stars overhead, the rocky trail in the circle of light in front of them, the ghost-like, stunted trees that would occasionally pop up nearby on the trail, and the bobbing of light from other hikers below and above them. Far down, Highway 395 and the Owens Valley showed a few lights from cars, homes, and stores, proving that civilization wasn't that distant.

After more steady climbing, James said, "I hope I can hike all the way to the summit. I'm already feeling tired and light-headed."

Mom sympathized with James. None of the Parkers had gotten enough sleep. "It's tricky to find your rhythm but I think it's best to take our minds off the trail," she suggested. "Try thinking of something else. Okay? I believe that will help, at least a little bit. I've been thinking of all the people who have been on this trek before us. Who was the first person to stand on top of Whitney? What were their thoughts? What will we be thinking later today when we are there? See if you can give it a try, okay?"

So, the nearly ten-year-old twins Morgan and James took Mom's advice. First, Morgan drifted back to about 2,400 years ago at the western side of the park, daydreaming of what it would have been like to be there then.

It was a beautiful early autumn morning 2,400 years ago. Sunshine
bathed a sprawling forest of massive sequoia trees. A recent fire, caused
by lightning, had scoured out large sections of trees and shrubs. The forest
floor was grayish black with ash, cleared from abundant underbrush and
many smaller trees.

Underneath a grove of large sequoias was a large swath of sequoia
cones, scattered about. Many of them had opened up due to the fire. A
single seed just the size of an oat flake from one of the egg-shaped cones
had settled onto fertile ground. In a nearby gully, water trickled down a
small stream.

Morgan thought it would soon be larger, replenished by winter rains
and snows.

She imagined standing there with her brother. They both focused on
that very special oatmeal flake-shaped seed. "It's in the perfect location,"
Morgan whispered reverently to James.

James surveyed the landscape. "Look at all that sunlight getting through
now because of the recent fire. And all that ash means added nutrients to
the soil. And, there's water nearby," James said, gesturing to the stream.

In a time-lapse sequence in her mind, Morgan watched the seed gradually open up. It soon sent a root down and a sprout pushed up. The sprout

then broke through the loose dirt covering it and it was now an incredibly small, baby sequoia. "Look!" Morgan called out excitedly to James, pointing to the brand-new tree.

Then Morgan spoke to the newborn sequoia. "I wish you a long, healthy, and happy life. And maybe I'll get to see you when you grow up!" She looked around the area and realized the brand-new tree was in the heart of the Giant Forest. She wondered, if the tree became a giant, what its name would be.

The twin Parkers continued to watch the tree as it grew larger and larger. Soon, after several years, it was a few feet high.

A deer came along one late spring morning, nibbling at the new-growth needles of several other conifers nearby. The deer wandered over to Morgan and James's special sequoia and bent over to feed on the grass at the base of the sapling.

Morgan and James each held their breath, knowing the deer needed to eat, and new needles on trees were its natural and often preferred diet. But still, they hoped the deer would find some other plant to nibble on.

"That sequoia is still so vulnerable," Morgan said, worried. "Deer feeding off a baby sequoia can kill the tree."

Then, for some reason, the deer trotted away, finding other plants to graze on.

"Whew!" James said. "The sequoia made it through another obstacle."

The sun peeked over the horizon to the east. Immediately, the stark, rocky terrain of the eastern Sierra was awash in sunlight. Morgan instantly snapped back to the present and turned off her flashlight. "I guess I don't need this anymore!" she said, putting it away.

Mom spoke to her daughter, "You've been awfully quiet for some time now."

Morgan smiled. "I just did what you said to do and took my mind off the trail. And guess what, it worked!"

James then said, "Where are we right now anyway?"

Dad gazed at the small lake far below them. "I think that's Mirror Lake down there. If I recall correctly, we're over four miles in."

In the now bright daylight, the family noticed, for the first time, that they had left a great deal of the plant life and almost all the trees behind. Dad announced, "We are well above 10,000 feet elevation now and soon will be passing tree line. Only seven more miles to go until the summit!"

Mom pointed at the glacially carved, U-shaped valley ahead toward Mount Whitney. "I know our destination is up there somewhere," she said.

Now, completely bathed in sunlight, the Parkers hiked on.

While struggling up the Mount Whitney Trail, Dad patted his belly and thought to himself, *I should have lost five pounds or so before hauling this extra weight up the mountain.* Dad looked up the trail as far as he could see. *I guess there's nothing I can do about that now,* he realized. The family continued hiking down several switchbacks. They moved slowly on the rocky terrain, their backpacks riding heavily on their hips and shoulders. Soon they were back in the shade of the deep forest. And after that, the giant trees were everywhere along the trail.

James and Morgan walked on, following their Mom and Dad on the rocky path. James, to take his mind off the extra-long hike, recalled something he heard on the Grant Grove talk about the early days of harvesting sequoias. He then imagined that he and Morgan were in Philadelphia for the Centennial Exhibition in 1876. . . .

Mom suddenly spoke, "Let's sit down here for a few minutes at Trailside Meadow. I think it's time for a little break."

The Parkers were now about halfway into their climb. It felt good to take a break, sitting on the rocks while Dad filtered water right next to the trail in Lone Pine Creek. Morgan and James lay down for the moment, their heads propped against a rock as a temporary pillow. "I'm really tired," James announced. "Can I just shut my eyes for a minute or two?"

Mom replied, "Just for a minute, okay? I'm afraid if we don't keep going we'll lose momentum and never make it to the top."

So, while James, Morgan, and Mom took a break, Dad filtered and filled several more water bottles with the creek so conveniently close.

The family lingered to rest at the lush (at least for the high elevation) trailside meadow.

Dad gazed upward along the seemingly never-ending trail. "We better get a move on," he said. The Parkers then quickly hiked into and through a part of the Whitney summit hike called Trail Camp. There, several tents were strewn about, placed by backpackers on sandy areas between granite rocks and boulders. But most of the camp-sites appeared empty— the people who set up the tents were likely on top of the peak or heading there. As the family hiked on, Mom said, "We could have stayed overnight, here, too. But I thought it best not to haul all that equipment up." Meanwhile, Dad picked up a few pieces of stray trash blowing about. He stuffed the garbage into a side pocket in his daypack. Morgan and James helped. "Some people," said Dad, "need to do a better job of keeping their campsites clean!"

Soon the Parkers approached the part of the hike they had been dreading the most, the famed ninety-nine switchbacks. This part of the climb seemed busy with peo-ple. But really it was just the zig-zagging trail—each turn brought hikers into view on the sections above and below. The switchbacks were relentless, and after a while, the family's enthusiasm and energy faded as they went on and on.

At one point, James stopped to take a deep breath. He hunched over then suddenly stood up, looking down the trail to see how far they had come. James noticed a body of water far below. "Hey look at that lake down there," he exclaimed, impressed by how much elevation they had gained.

James took a moment to look up what lake it was on his map. He pulled the map out of his daypack. "It's Consultation Lake," James announced. "I wonder why it got named that."

Morgan paused to guzzle almost half of a large container of water. The high elevation and bright sunshine as well as the stress of the hike was making her thirstier than she could ever remember. She looked up at her family who were itching to continue their climb to the top of the mountain. James took a long drink from his canteen and then called out, "Let's keep going Morgan!"

"Hang on," Mom replied. "There's no need to hurry, and we all need as much water as we can handle."

Morgan took one more gulp then looked up. She saw hikers on several bends in the trail above them, "It's still just one switchback after another," she said. "I think we must have done this over a hundred times."

"Then we should be just about done," Dad replied. "There are supposed to be ninety-nine switchbacks here."

Morgan felt a sense of urgency to keep the momentum of the incredible hike moving forward. She closed the water bottle and stuffed it into her daypack. Then she scampered up to her family and announced, playfully, "What are you all waiting for?"

13

Eventually, the Parkers came to a stretch of cables bolted into the mountain. The area above and below this section of trail was steep and rocky. The cables were needed to prevent slips and falls. Mom took the lead. She held onto the first cable then peered down into the steep chute below. Then she gazed ahead at a few intermittent snow patches still clinging to the cliff-like areas close to the trail.

"It may be August," Mom announced, "but we have some steep, icy sections ahead. We're going to go slowly and one at a time, and always stay close together. Please use the cables for a steady grip along the way. Also watch your footing and stay right on the center of the trail. I don't want anyone stepping near the cliff or on the steep sections of ice and snow farther up. This whole section is dangerous and I want to make sure we take our time with each step."

Mom looked at her family and began walking. Slowly the Parkers followed Mom

along the cables. About halfway in and without any mishaps, everyone's confidence grew and they each took slightly quicker steps.
They passed a few spots where ice covered the trail. Following the
footsteps of others before them, this part of the trail proved less
difficult than anticipated.

Then the family stepped out of the cabled section and back
onto the trail. "Well," Mom sighed and smiled at her family. "That's
a relief, except we have to go back down the same way later. In the
shade during the late afternoon, some of the snow may get iced over
by then." Mom paused for a moment then added, "I guess we'll just
deal with that when we come back this way."

It was well into the day by now and bright sunshine was blasting
down. The area the family was in was completely void of trees and
totally rock-bound. There were jagged, pinnacled peaks above, but
not much higher in elevation. In front, Mom gazed at what lie ahead.
She turned to her family and announced with excitement, "We are
almost there folks!"

"How is everyone doing?" Dad asked from the back.

"I have to admit, I am getting light-headed," Mom said. "But I can
go on."

"I know I should eat, but I'm really not hungry. I wish I was,"
James added.

"I'm tired. Can we sit and rest for a while?" Morgan pleaded, but
then added, "It's okay, I can keep going."

Hearing all this, Mom became worried. Was the trail getting the
best of everyone? She wondered if they should they call it quits and
say, like many, "We tried to summit Whitney but it was too much for
us and we turned around somewhere over 13,000 feet." Finally,
Mom said, "Why don't we take a short snack break here?"

Quickly everyone found a makeshift seat on some rocks. They
dug in their packs and soon were nibbling on raisins, nuts,
and granola bars. No one felt very hungry, but the food
provided a shot of energy.

Soon, everyone stood up to start hiking again. But
just getting up was painstakingly slow and difficult.

14

While trudging closer and closer to the summit, Dad suddenly announced. "Only two and a half miles to go!"

"And less than 1,000 feet of elevation gain," Mom added. Then she looked at her tired family. "It's late morning and we have been up for over ten hours already. Did any of us really sleep well last night?"

Mom paused a second, gauging whether the twins and she and Robert were capable to go on. She knew that tired hikers are more likely to make mistakes and get hurt. But the trail now was well worn and heavily travelled, putting some of Mom's persistent safety concerns at ease. Then she looked toward the top of the mountain. "What do you think everyone? Press on?"

Everyone agreed that from this point it was definitely worth finishing the trip. But before they did, Morgan snapped several pictures at Trail Crest. Then she asked a backcountry ranger to take one of the whole family. Morgan handed her the camera. The ranger looked into the lens and said, jokingly, "Oh, it looks like all of you just started out. There's plenty left in the tank to hike on, right?"

Morgan took her camera back. Then the family gazed at the lakes and snowfields far below them, and the summit not too far ahead. Dad urged everyone on. "Let's go!" he called out. And with that the Parkers surged toward the top.

At that point, for a very short distance, the Mount Whitney Trail actually went downhill a bit. Mom said, "That might be nice, now, but on the way down, we'll have to go up a little and that might be pretty difficult. Our legs are going to be awfully tired by then!"

But the Parkers slogged on and made it to their next goal, the John Muir Trail junction. The sign noted that they had less than two miles to go.

The family paused and drank some more water. Dad spontaneously took both backpacks from the twins and stuffed them into his. "I've got these the rest of the way," he said. Morgan and James smiled and didn't say a word in protest.

The view was amazing. There were deep, U-shaped glacially carved valleys, spired peaks, and far to the west, distant forests. James and Morgan stared in that direction. Then James whispered to Morgan, "The General Sherman tree is out there somewhere."

Morgan replied, jokingly, "I guess it isn't that big then because we can't see it from here."

Mom ended the brief conversation. "C'mon. We should keep going."

Getting started again after stopping was once again slow and difficult. The family had lost some momentum, and walking at this elevation, after exerting so much energy for so long, was a struggle. Hikers were now consistently passing the Parkers. And doubt returned to each of them. "Are we going to make it?" each thought.

A couple came up behind the family and slowed down. The trail at that point was on angled slabs of rock and there was no safe place to pass. Finally at a less precarious spot, Dad ushered his family to the side and let the faster hikers go by. But the couple stopped anyway. The man looked at the twins with astonishment. "How old are you two?" he asked.

Morgan answered "We turn ten in two months."

"Twins?" the man asked.

"Yep," James replied.

"Exhausted twins," Mom said for them.

Then the man looked at the whole family. "I have to tell you something. This is my twelfth time summiting Whitney. I don't think I've ever seen someone so young get so far. Congratulations are in order!"

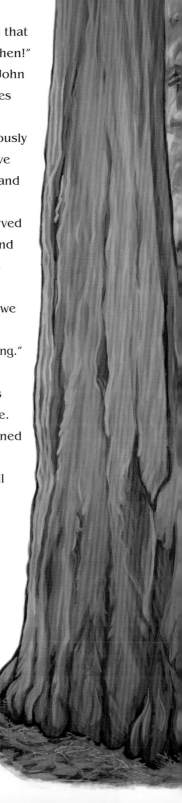

The man high-fived Morgan and James and said good-bye to the family. As he and his partner hiked on, he turned back over his shoulder and called out. "Don't quit now. You are almost to the top and the hardest part is behind you!"

The praise gave Morgan and James a second wind and they hiked on with another surge of energy.

While walking, James looked up at the blaring, immensely blue sky. "I've never seen the sky so dark blue," he said.

"That's because we've never been at this high an elevation," Dad replied.

"You mean James and I have never been at this elevation," Morgan responded. "You and Mom climbed the Grand Teton."

Mom replied, "The Grand Teton was just a few feet higher up than where we are right now and we're going to pass that elevation very soon."

"How's everyone doing?" Dad asked. "Any altitude issues? Dizziness? Light-headed? Tired? Hungry?"

"All of the above," James admitted, with a chuckle. "But I can keep on going."

"I don't feel like eating anything," Morgan added. "Even though I know I am supposed to."

"We do have to keep our food intake up," Mom said. "We need the calories and energy whether we realize it or not. But we're making great time and it's a perfect day for going on."

Mom insisted everyone drink more water. Then she handed out energy bars that the family nibbled on while hiking. Realizing how well everyone suddenly appeared to be doing, Mom said, "I think all our days of camping and hiking above 6,000 feet helped acclimate us for this high-elevation jaunt today."

In the warming part of the day, the Parkers shed some of their cold-weather clothes and continued on.

15

Bright sunlight bouncing off the rocks baked Morgan and the rest of the Parkers. Wearing a cap and sunglasses, she squinted as she looked up the trail toward Mount Whitney's summit, now clearly in view. Morgan pushed the brim of her hat down lower on her face. She also nudged her sunglasses closer in, reducing the glare just a little bit. Then she hiked on with the rest of her family.

The Parkers now traversed through a corridor where slots between mountain walls acted like windows where they could see far below and beyond to the horizon. Mom took the lead and peered over one such vantage point and said, "We are way up high now!"

And they all knew they were getting close. Morgan gazed toward the top of the mountain and called out, "There are hikers up there."

The trail even leveled out some, increasing the family's pace as they approached the celebrated high-elevation peak. Shade would be nice right now, James thought, as he looked at the rock-bound world he was in.

On their final stretch to the top of Mount Whitney, desire took over. Once the Parkers got close enough, they could see people milling about on the summit. They also saw one more thing that indicated to the family they were just about done climbing. "There's the hut on the top of the mountain!" Morgan called out. "It looks just like the picture in the guidebook."

The last few steps to the top were slow, but not as slow as they had been. The last part of the trail was almost level, but they were also approaching 14,500 feet. When

realizing the numbers, Dad said, "Just think, if we were on Mount Everest we'd be about halfway to the top!"

Finally, the family conquered the last few feet and it was clear there was no more uphill left to climb. The Parkers celebrated by circling around the summit marker on top of Mount Whitney. The small round piece of metal was embedded in the rock just like the one the family had seen earlier on the top of Little Baldy. The Parkers stood there hugging and high fiving each other and turning 360 degrees to take in the full, awe-inspiring view from the peak.

With her phone, Morgan grabbed video of their time on the summit while interviewing each person in the family.

James scanned the incredible view. "It's all rocks up here and a few tiny patches of snow with some lakes far below," he said. "We are way above tree line."

Morgan added, "And we thought Little Baldy was high up. We are 6,500 feet higher than that right now. The world below looks like it does from an airplane."

Mom continued, "It's definitely a 360-degree view from here. We can gaze all the way down to the Owens Valley more than 10,000 feet below us. Also, looking west we can see the area where the Giant Forest is and all the sequoias, but it is too hazy and far away to make them out from this distance." Mom then thought for a moment. "Oh yeah, we couldn't see Mount Whitney from Moro Rock, so we likely can't see the Giant Forest from here."

Dad reported, as if he was being interviewed for something like the Discovery Channel, "It's an amazing day on the Mount Whitney summit. We are arriving in early afternoon after hiking half the night and all morning, which was right about how much time we estimated the climb would take. There's a light breeze blowing but it's not too strong and there's not a single cloud in the sky. The sun is blaring down on all of us and the sky is the deepest blue I think I have ever seen. My family and I are perched on rocks on what feels like the top of the world."

James wrote:

This is James Parker reporting.

Sequoia and Kings Canyon are amazing. And we live so close to both of them. Our home in San Luis Obispo is only three or four hours away! I plan on coming back to both parks for the rest of my life—in winter and summer. We saw so much this time, but there is so much more left to see. And I really want to go backpacking here, for five days or even longer.

My top ten sights for Sequoia and Kings Canyon National Parks are:

1) Mist Falls
2) Bears
3) Tokopah Falls
4) Crystal Cave
5) Little Baldy Summit
6) Moro Rock
7) Mineral King
8) General's Highway between the parks
9) Zumwalt Meadow
10) On top of Mount Whitney

The Parkers took several pictures then asked another hiker to take a few pictures of all of them together. They saw scores of other hikers up there, too, but eventually found their own place on some rocks to sit and soak it all in.

After eating, Mom and Dad took a few moments to walk around and talk to others on the summit that day. They learned that some made the climb in one day, just like the Parkers. Others had spread the hike out over two or three days at a much more relaxed pace, backpacking and camping along the way. And, still some made the trek as part of a long journey, with a few coming along the John Muir Trail all the way from Yosemite Valley, well over 200 miles away!

For some, the Parkers learned it was their first time on the mountain. For others, it was one of many return trips. The youngest people everyone saw on Whitney that day were clearly Morgan and James. "I am so proud of you," Mom said at one point to the twins. "That was some serious hiking!" And the oldest on the mountain, at least of the people the Parkers met, was an eighty-one-year-old man returning for the first time in twenty-five years! Morgan took a photo with him at the summit. "I'll share it online with you once we get back home," she said.

Eventually, Morgan and James pulled out their journals, packed along in daypacks for the hike.

After a magnificent few hours on the summit walking around, taking short naps, and sketching in their journals, it was midafternoon and a stiff breeze picked up. The Parkers quickly dug in their daypacks and pulled on lightweight jackets.

Then Dad stood up stiffly, stretched, and looked at the still clear-blue sky. "Well, what goes up must come down," he announced. And with that, the family began their long journey back down the mountain.

Morgan wrote:

From the Top of the World,

You know how your parents always ask you what you want to be when you grow up? Well, after visiting here I want to be a national park ranger—and work in this park. I want to be around these trees, helping them, for as long as I can. I do wonder though, if pollution or climate change is getting to them. I certainly hope not. My top ten list for the two parks is mostly about the trees. Here goes:

1) General Grant Tree
2) Tharp's Log
3) General Sherman Tree
4) Redwood Canyon
5) Giant Forest
6) Log Meadow and the bears
7) Moro Rock
8) Converse Basin and the Boole Tree
9) Giant Forest Museum
10) The summit of Mount Whitney

Epilogue

Early one Sunday in December, Morgan and James were sleeping in. But not for long.

Mom and Dad snuck into Morgan and James's bedrooms and woke them up. They said to the twins that they needed to get dressed. They had plans.

Morgan said sleepily, "Where are we going?"

"It's a surprise," Mom answered. "But we have a good little journey ahead of us, so we have to head out now."

Nearly three hours after leaving their California coastal city of San Luis Obispo behind, the Parkers pulled into the Chamber of Commerce parking lot in the San Joaquin Valley town of Sanger. There they loaded onto one of several chartered buses with scores of other people. Once everyone was on board, drinks and pastries were given to all.

Soon the buses were heading into the foothills. It was then that both Morgan and James started to get an inkling of what lay ahead. "I remember this highway," Morgan said. "I bet we're on our way to the sequoias!"

"I think we're heading back to Kings Canyon!" James exclaimed. "To see the trees in winter covered in snow."

Mom and Dad heard the twins talking and smiled. Dad said, "Ever since we left the two parks last summer, I have been wanting to come back."

One of the guides announced to the passengers, "We will be arriving in Grant Grove very soon!"

Morgan nearly shouted, "Grant Grove! That's where we were last summer! The General Grant Tree is there. Yeah!"

The twins now beamed at their parents.

The announcements continued. "Once we get there, we'll head straight to

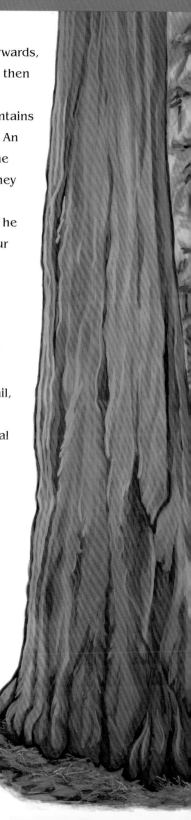

the General Grant Tree. Our ceremony will begin right away. Afterwards, there will be time to play in the snow, walk the wintery trails, and then meet at the lodge for a traditional holiday dinner."

The road continued to climb and they were clearly in the mountains now. Fresh snow lined the highway and adorned the tall conifers. An occasional giant sequoia grew close to the highway. Eventually, the bus pulled into Kings Canyon National Park. A short while later, they were in the Grant Grove parking lot.

James stared out the window at the snow-covered trees. Then he turned to his parents and said, "You brought us back to one of our all-time favorite places!"

Once the bus stopped, Morgan and James waited patiently to get off. They were incredibly eager to get to see their old friend, the General Grant. When they were all properly bundled up for the cold air, the family exited the bus. The parking lot was mostly cleared, with piles of snow off to the side where they had been pushed up by snowplows. But as soon as everyone was on the trail, it was all snow. The Parkers, and all the others, followed the foot-prints of those who had gone before them. And despite the several feet of snow on the ground, Morgan and James raced up to the second largest tree in the world.

It was exhilarating to be back at the General Grant Tree, espe-cially to see it adorned with snow. The whole forest was covered with large pillows of snow draped on many tree branches. It was a perfect holiday scene, like one right out of a postcard!

As she caught her breath at the base of the giant tree, Morgan said, "I can see why they call it the Nation's Christmas Tree now. You don't even need ornaments to make it look so beautiful for the season."

James joked in reply, "It sure wouldn't fit in our living room."

The crowd gathered there, with many taking seats in chairs facing the tree, a musical band, and a choir ready to sing. A ranger stepped forward. The Parkers

immediately recognized her as Colleen, the ranger from last summer. She saw Morgan and James right away and said. "Hey! It's my old buddies. It is so good to see you."

"It's good to see you, too," James replied. "I'm surprised you remember us though, with all the visitors you must get. But it is also fantastic to be back in the park during a whole new season."

Colleen stood in front and greeted the large crowd. "Welcome to all of you on this brisk, winter's day at 6,500 feet. Thank you so much for making this journey, as so many people have done since the early 1900s, to see this great tree in winter. Many of you may have seen our giant sequoias in summer, but it's a whole new world up here in December. And with the drought we've been having, it is awesome to have some fresh snow on the ground!"

Colleen smiled at everyone and then continued, "The General Grant Tree is the Nation's Christmas Tree. To start our ceremony, I am going to lay this wreath right at the base of the General Grant, just as we have done for years." Colleen placed a large, decorated holiday wreath up against the General Grant. Then she said, "This wreath is

placed here in memory of our soldiers and those who served and gave their lives to our country." Colleen purposefully was silent for a moment then changed the subject. "We have a lot of fun activities for you today and I want us to get right to it. First off, the Sanger High School Band will accompany the Sanger Community Choir and lead us in several Christmas carols."

The choir up front faced the crowd. Their director led them in singing while the band played along. Everyone sang along, with puffs of steam coming out of their mouths.

Morgan thought in between verses, *how cool this is to be at the best place in the United States to kick off the holidays.*

James thought, *Singing is great but I can't wait to play in the snow after.*

Mom thought, *I need to get back into a choir. I just love this.*

And Dad thought, *We are so lucky to be here, what a great event this is, but my stomach is kind of growling. I can't wait for that holiday meal!*

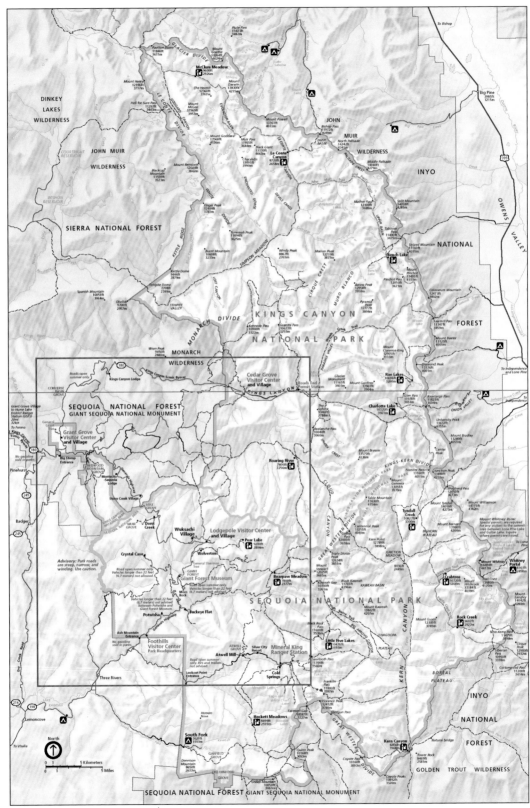

* Purple box shows roaded area of the parks.

About the Author

MIKE GRAF is a part time television weathercaster and a former elementary school teacher and university professor. He has shared his writing and national park experiences with children and teachers in hundreds of schools. Mike has published more than ninety fiction and nonfiction books for children and teachers. He visits many national parks each year, but often comes to Sequoia and Kings Canyon National Parks and has been going to those two parks all his life. Mike lives with his wife and daughter in Chico, California.